A Collection of Poetry with a Sprinkling of Short Stories

Volume 1

by

Rosy Gee

ISBN-13: 9798767695508

I dedicate this book to my beautiful daughter, Rachel,
because without her unwavering support and encouragement,
it would never have materialised.
Shall I compare thee to a summer's day?
Yes, because you light up my life just like a summer's day.

CONTENTS

The Colour of My Skin 1

Autumn Glory 3

No One Knows 4

An English Country Garden 6

The Castle 7

Breaking Up is Hard To Do 8

The Water Mill 10

The Tree of Life 11

Crashing Waves 12

Beach Bay Day 13

Against All Odds 14

Stepping Back in Time 16

The Axe Man 20

The Orchid Plant 21

The Golden Egg 23

Love Consumed 27

The Bird Club 28

Hot Air Balloon 31

Double Trouble 32

Motherhood 37

Sunshine and Showers 38

Glorious Spring 39

Reflections 41

Baking Day 46

A Chance Encounter 48

Do Not Hurt Me, I am Too Weak 58

Peace of Mind 59

The Summer of 1974 60

Unconditional Love 63

Cursed 64

Memories 72

The Woman in Black 74

Release Me 78

Daybreak 79
Watching Over Us 80
Shadows 84
Castles in the Sand 85
We Are One 90
To Have and To Hold 91
The Magic Kingdom 94
ABOUT THE AUTHOR 101

ACKNOWLEDGEMENTS

I would like to thank my publishing team for guiding me through the process of producing this book. I am a writer and love writing; I do not have the time or the inclination to edit, format and ultimately publish my work. They were wonderfully supportive and professional throughout and I will always be indebted to them for launching my debut collection.

The Colour of My Skin

Work-worn hands weathered by time
Decades of lifting, holding, loving
Hoisting children skywards, then
With the passage of time, blessed
To be able to hoist my children's children
High into the sky, happy, innocent and free

My eyes have seen and witnessed so much
During the course of a full life
Wars raging in far-flung places
Droughts, famine, suffering and pain
The blood runs freely through my veins
Coursing easily and unfettered

Riots and unrest; civilians outraged
At acts of violence metered out
Unnecessary inequalities and hatred
Instilled over time, ingrained so deep
But why? The colour of my skin
Has no reflection on me being me

Actions and words spoken; compassion shown
To my fellow man – a warm smile, a handshake
In gratitude and appreciation of work done
Or time given freely in acts of genuine kindness
The true nature of our souls will always shine through
The colour of our skin

Autumn Glory

Bronze, scarlet and burnished gold
Curly, crisp and meek to fold
Cascades of colour brightly adorn
Thresholds of each fresh new morn

Softly, silently, pearl-drops of dew
Whispering gently to revive the hue
Alas, in vain they glisten so fresh
Upon those crippled fingers of flesh

Wiry gauntlets piercing grey skies
Beguiled, bespangled, heavenwards rise
Mystical, chanting on sombre key
Ablaze with rustic anonymity

Those brazen sprays of lacy leaves
Dance in earnest upon the breeze
Trunks twisted, gnarled and grey
The splendours of an autumnal day

No One Knows

Drinking vessel proffered; grime-clogged nails
Styrofoam rigid, white, static
Stark against the dinginess of the stairwell
Matted head, stooped, unseeing, bowed low
In shame, disgust, distaste? No one knows

A penny, small and brown, sits alone
Like its owner, isolated, hopeless
Hunched on the stairwell, cold and hungry
Shoppers bustle to and fro, heads bowed
In shame, disgust, distaste? No one knows

A thousand pairs of feet must have passed
Sneakers, brogues, stilettoed toes painted red
Hurrying, scurrying. To where? No one knows
A myriad of things to do, people to see
Some choosing not to see what's at their feet

Laughter tinkles around the bar, glasses chink
A good day's work in the city, well rewarded
Fat cats dine, wine pours down their well-lubricated throats
Outside, hunched on the stairwell, head bowed
In shame, disgust, distaste? No one knows

Cut-glass, angular, high-rise and flying
Multi-million-dollar deals cut ice
Solitary penny in the Styrofoam cup
Her Majesty's profile glinting in the midday sun
A London bus clogs the cloying grime to choking point

An English Country Garden

Lengthening shadows cast mystical shapes on freshly mown
lawns
Magical moments; arenas bathed in dappled hues
The heat of the day dissipated as evening descends
On an English country garden
Fragrant blooms bow their heads in silent appreciation
The shimmering heat of the day subsides into a tranquil hush
Save for the distant warbling of a solitary songbird
Piercing the silence with its enchanting call

The Castle

Staunch the turrets stand, stark, grey bare;
Towering high, cold, mean into the wintry air,
Fickle fingers of fortress reaching high,
Sinister silhouettes against a midnight sky.

Noble, its arches bow, protecting within;
Soldiers fought to save kith and kin,
And together they battled, bitter and strong,
Until slowly crushed by the advancing throng.

Stones of ages past, each a story to tell,
Torture seeping through in each a hell,
Now, tranquillity reigns, an owl quietly calls,
Chaos of battles past ingrained deep in its walls.

Throughout the years seasons ebbed and flowed,
Warm sunlight baked the earth where cattle once lowed;
Sublime, inanimate, never to be beat,
It stands in all its glory, a wondrous feat

Breaking Up is Hard To Do

Y ou know when the time has come to end a relationship. You can feel it, deep inside. It is going to hurt, even though it is your decision to end it all.

There are many reasons a relationship fails. It's the little things that add up. I once compared my long-term marriage ending to the lights going out in a tower block, floor by floor.

As newlyweds, the block of 100 floors were brightly illuminated for many years. Then, one by one, the floors fell into darkness until there was just one floor remaining. The night these lights were extinguished, my marriage ended. Like a candle being snuffed out.

It took strength and courage to announce it to those concerned. I was blowing my comfortable life to smithereens and all those in it, including children.

Back to my current relationship. It was love at first sight. I cannot deny that. The frisson of excitement that I felt was overwhelming. We didn't go through the 'honeymoon period' – we didn't need to. It was love at first sight. That was two years ago.

I honestly thought it would last a lot longer than it did. I guess the tower block lights started to go out faster this time around. I felt a maelstrom of emotions spinning me with such a centrifugal force that I came tumbling down to earth with a bang and I realised that I had made a terrible mistake. A bad misjudgement.

With my two previous relationships, the decision was mine to break up. I'm not proud of that, it's just the way that it was. I am not afraid to step into the abyss and if I am not happy, I will take action and find a resolution. Life's too short.

This time it wasn't particularly difficult but I had still reached my conclusion: the relationship had to end. This lady was not for turning.

She doesn't know yet. I need to find the right time – whenever that is. All I know is that I cannot go on like this. She must see that, surely? She can't still think that I have feelings for her? She must have noticed my coolness towards her, the way I don't caress her beautiful curves as lovingly as I used to, or as often.

In the past, I have tackled things head-on, but this time I'm taking the coward's way out.

I have opted to be away the day the low-loader is scheduled to pick up my beautiful, fast, amazing car that I have loved unconditionally. She sits on my driveway while I beaver away in my home office and completely ignore her.

Sometimes, I have to take her out for a drive just to keep her happy. Crazy! It saddens me deeply to say this, but I do not need her any longer and I must let her go.

I will have a tear in my eye the day she leaves.

The Water Mill

A solitary workhorse amid leafy waters
The ancient wheel turns lifting, grinding, creaking
A million gallons flowing through its innards
Gushing, bubbling, cascading downwards
Carving smooth mosaics out of rugged rocks
Silken slate moulding moss-edged riverbanks
Perpetuating life through time
Carving life-lines into teeming riverbeds
Fern-clipped banks wait in misted hush
Wild garlic-scented air stilled by time
Shimmering against the pink-grey plumage
Of a lazy wood pigeon quivering
As he surveys the wooded banks amid leafy grandeur
The river winds its way endlessly on through time

The Tree of Life

The mighty gnarled and twisted bones of a majestic oak
Seeded from a tiny acorn towering skywards, glorious
Structured strong and outstretched, spanning decades
Hushed in the breeze listening and watching, forming the
landscape

Life as a sapling struggling for traction, buffeted by wind and rain
Centuries passed slowly sifting through its leaves, branches and
nooks
Ragged bark against a cerulean blue sky stretching up to greet
the sun
As horses and carriages passed beneath in regal splendour

Squirrels, woodpeckers, pigeons, crows, insects and spiders
Made it their home to feast, rear young, sit, perch, eat and listen
To the landscape of nature's mantle spread beneath them
Awash with the vibrancy of life, invisible, frenetic

And silently time seeped by in, round and through the seasons
One by one, year by year, decades turning into centuries
As time stood still when the tree withered and crumbled
Racked by storms and lightning it surrendered, leaving a stark
tomb

Crashing Waves

Crashing waves break; calling
Over and over taunting me
A sea-spray of emotions tumbling
As I ebb and flow on the shoreline

Torn this way and that, blinded
By time, black clouds scudding
As tears prickle my eyes
Sadness overwhelms me

Fresh rain on asphalt sizzles
Through my brain like fire
And mystical dancers pirouette
On the knife edge of my life

Cigarette butt stubbed and heart heavy
I wander aimlessly staring out at the ocean
Pulling me like a magnet
Will I do the right thing?

Beach Bay Day

Diamantes sparkle, dapple and dance
Across the magical sea-scaped bay
Surfers catching a wave, curling
Living the dream on a hazy summer's day
Cool dudes, ripped bodies, slicked-back hair
VW vans line the slipway; music thumps
Children play, dogs pant attentive to their owners'
Ice-cream licking tongues waiting for a drip to drop
In the blazing heat of the afternoon sun
An English summer's day seared into our memories
Forever, as we entwine on the harsh, concrete breakwater
Feeling the sun kiss our skin, tingling in the salty sea air
Relishing and drinking in, the sandy beach bay day

Against All Odds

Sombre seaside towns huddle miserably on morning tides
Where bobbing infants once dotted the placid green swell
But overhead, silent thick clouds skim leaden skies
And foaming waves shun naked bays but for scrawny gulls
Squawking into brittle winds as they spiral upwards
Desperate in their search for food they shuttle to nearby land
But the jaded landscape lies pallid and weak, devoid of warmth
As frantic farmers gather failing crops amid silent depression
Against all odds

When harvesting was once a happy time, now a menial task
They scratch the land for winter feed melancholy in their
search
Amid quagmires of filth awash with the stench of despair
No rewards for their sweat and toil, only dank dark clouds
Releasing deluges on already sodden pastures
Where fat stock once chewed cud lazily in the blistering heat
Swatting flies with heavy tails as sword-like swallows swooped
Filling their snowy bibs above the dew-drenched meadows
Sprinkled with the salt-and-pepper of sweet clover heads
Awaiting new-born calves to cushion their soft warm bodies
Against all odds

But the heavens opened up and clouds obscured the morning
sun
Taking with it memories; leaving behind scarred bitter remarks
From kindly old gents who once enjoyed a friendly game of
bowls
And scanned soft green pitches for signs of victory
From grandsons proud and erect, battling to win, pure and
innocent
In their quest to impress their loved ones watching on
Against all odds

No lanterns of foaming blooms cascading on open doors
Of idyllic thatched cottages edging narrow country lanes
Where roses once encased oak doors in frameworks of pastel
beauty
And sweet old ladies took tea on manicured lawns
Trimmed with flounces of lavender and delphiniums
Sheltering wise eyes from the afternoon sun with frail hands
Now they too reminisce from cosy fire-side chairs as
Cruel easterly winds bitterly crush those delicate summer
blooms
Against all odds

Stepping Back in Time

Angus side-stepped some brambles overhanging the footpath which ran alongside the railway track. It was late spring and his mind was a jumble of divorce petition statements, financial outgoings, and worrying whether his wife would take him to the cleaners and ruin his successful estate agency business.

Laura had told him often that she would ruin him and the more she said it, the more determined Angus was to stop her. Seventeen years of marriage and three children later and it had finally come to this.

One minute they were all loved-up and couldn't keep their hands off each other and the next, a pedestrian lifestyle had settled around them like an obscure fog, almost suffocating them in its dull routine. He had worked all hours building up the business and Laura had worked tirelessly in the background, running a home, organising the children, and helping with the accounts most evenings.

As the path opened up ahead of him, Angus enjoyed the view across the marshland and watched as a heron squawked and flew up, its lumbering, grey wings and long, spindly legs silhouetted against the clear blue sky above him.

His heart was heavy and the thought of going back to the cottage he had rented until the divorce was finalised, filled him with dread – it was cramped and dark, but it was preferable to

having another slanging match with Laura in their marital home a short drive away. She had lost her sparkle and was constantly moaning or tired. She sounded like a stuck record: 'When can you take the kids to school?' or, 'You've missed every Parent-Teacher evening this year.'

He was still trying to figure out when his marriage had started to go so wrong when he noticed a young woman, her long blonde hair billowing in the soft breeze, standing in the centre of the small railway bridge that crossed the track just ahead of him. He could hear the train in the distance approaching with its familiar 'dunkety-dunkety-dunk' rhythm on the tracks.

Horrified, he watched as she clambered up onto the parapet and stood with her arms outstretched like Christ the Redeemer. He broke into a sprint and as he approached the bridge, he could hear the train getting louder and louder.

Running as fast as his legs would carry him, Angus reached the base of the steps and flew up them two at a time until he reached the top and was standing, breathless, a few feet away from the desperate woman.

"Hey!" he called softly. "Don't jump! Please, wait."

As he spoke, he walked calmly towards her with his arms outstretched. His heart was pounding and his mouth was so dry, he had difficulty speaking.

"Please. Come down," he begged, his voice full of compassion.

She wavered when he spoke and stared ahead of her down the tracks. The train was rounding the bend and hurtling towards them. Angus wanted to make a grab for her but was afraid she would lose her balance and fall.

Everything seemed to happen in slow motion and the woman stepped back and dropped like a stone. Angus managed to break her fall and caught her as he landed on top of her, covering her protectively with his body. He held her tight as the train thundered past beneath them, vibrating the whole bridge as it sped through, the noise deafening them both.

The woman was sobbing and a small crowd was rubbernecking to see what was going on.

"It's alright," Angus announced calmly. "She's okay. Just give us some space," he told them authoritatively.

Slowly, he helped the woman to her feet and their eyes locked.

It was Laura.

"Christ, Laura. What were you thinking?" he asked, visibly shaken.

"I'm sorry, Angus," she whispered between sobs. "I just couldn't go on."

He was shocked. Had he driven her to this? Was it his fault?

He was holding her shoulders firmly in his hands and looking into her face.

"Come on. Let's get you home. Nothing is ever that bad. Do you hear me? We'll get through this."

She nodded, robotic and stunned, her eyes smudged and streaked with mascara.

"I'll take care of you. I promise," he said, taking her gently into his arms.

The Axe Man

White-coated man, reverent and hushed
Insipidly gestures with a monotone voice
Over his frail body, ravaged with pain
Realisation trickles through; it is time

Hunched at a window, he watches the world go by
A world that has no place for him
I rest my head against his
My tears are salty and deep

We smile at each other, our words unspoken
His courage and dignity sears into my soul
Autumn closes in on us both
The full bloom of summer is fading fast

Poised, the axe man waits mercilessly
Silhouetted against the blackening sky
Mocking, jeering, haunting,
Glorious in his power. Helpless, we wait

His furrowed brow is no longer furrowed
As the threads of life fall away one by one
The axe man's job is done; he labours no more
The suffering is over. The axe man has gone

The Orchid Plant

Presented with a flourish
The exquisite, exotic flowers
Blushed pink delicate veined and
Cheetah-spotted throats
Hung on tender stems
Tilted to the light, bathed in beauty
Flushed with expectation

A young girl on the cusp of womanhood
Dancing in the moonlit-bathed arena
Of life so promising and full of love
Catches her breath as he takes her
Tenderly into his arms, melting her
Against him, a snapshot of their future
Enshrined in their hearts forever

Foal-like limbs strengthen and mature
Her boyish figure blossoms into full bloom
Sensual, full-lipped, round-breasted
Arches of lust and love, she ripens
Beneath the cherry-rich pickings of
The fruits of her loins, expectant and
Hungry for the touch of his skin on hers

Rheumy-eyed and arthritic hands move
Slowly to the swaying rhythm of time
As the orchid plant is gently lifted so carefully
So as not to break the delicate stems
Which hang heavy with exotic blooms
Their faces tilted to the sun, a picture of serenity
The exquisite flowers cause her to smile sweetly

The Golden Egg

Miranda watched proudly as her seven-year-old daughter, Kitty, rummaged among the bushes in search of an Easter egg that she had hidden earlier for the hunt. Kitty's twin cousins, Lily and Leo, were scampering around the garden searching for the other eggs.

It was a warm, spring day in Brighton, the coastal town in the south of England, and Miranda hugged herself as she watched the children darting around in their hunt for the hidden treasures.

"Tea?" Bev stepped out onto the patio through the bi-fold doors which led into Miranda's amazing kitchen. She handed a porcelain mug to her sister containing camomile tea.

Miranda took it, smiling. "Thanks."

The sisters sat down on the swing chair overlooking the garden.

"The house looks fantastic!" Bev enthused. "You've done a great job."

"Oh, the architects and interior designers should take all the credit. I just told them what I wanted and they did all the rest."

"Well, hats off to you, sis. It's turned out better than I could ever have imagined. It looks so modern and spacious and lovely and light, bright and airy. I'm envious." She stopped short and took a sip of her coffee.

"All in good time, Bev. Rome wasn't built in a day."

Bev sighed. "I know, but Ray is always so busy at work, he's never got time to do anything around the house and we can't afford to get people in. Especially now." She rubbed her rounded belly absent-mindedly.

Miranda looked away. "Who's ready for the next clue?" she called out.

The twins were squealing with delight as they had found another egg hidden in a flower pot next to the potting shed.

Kitty looked crestfallen and as she did a little skip, her green tartan skirt flapped in the breeze. Her cream woollen tights and matching cardigan made her look like a little pixie and Miranda's heart melted.

"OK. Listen up! I stand in rivers on one leg and wait for my supper to swim by."

Kitty got it straight away and made a beeline for the life-sized heron sculpture that her dad had given her mum for her birthday last year. With the twins hot on her heels, Kitty rummaged around the base among the herbaceous plants and eventually jumped up with a bright pink foil-wrapped egg.

"I found it!" she squealed, popping it into the tiny basket Miranda had given to each of the children before the hunt.

"One last clue, then. Whoever solves this will win the Easter bunny!"

By this time, all three children were sifting through the vegetation looking for more hidden treasures. Auntie Miranda

always hid loads of eggs and Kitty knew that there was always plenty of chocolates to go round.

"Are you and Michael going to try again?" Bev asked tentatively, feeling guilty at how quickly she had fallen pregnant after deciding to have another child.

Miranda's face went taut. "No. I don't think I can cope with another miscarriage. Besides, Kitty will be eight in July, and…" Her voice trailed off as she looked wistfully at her sister's swollen tummy.

"Kitty will have to be an only child, I'm afraid. It's not what Michael and I wanted, but that's just the way things have turned out. Besides, look at her. Isn't she beautiful?"

Bev smiled. Kitty was a real character and a delightful little girl.

"Come on, gather round!" Lily, Leo, and Kitty ran towards Miranda and grouped around excitedly at her feet, wide-eyed with anticipation. "We need these in the winter to keep us warm, but they have all gone."

The children conferred and Leo piped up, "I know! The log store!" The children scampered off down to the wood store where Miranda had lovingly hidden the end prize.

The sisters watched on as the three little ones each found a beautiful fluffy Easter bunny, exquisitely gift-wrapped holding a gigantic golden Easter egg in its paws.

"You spoil them," Bev chided.

Miranda smiled. "You watch the children. I'll go and start prepping for the barbecue for when the guys get back. I'll expect they'll be hungry after their round of golf."

"Yes. Thirsty, too, I expect."

"I've put plenty of beers in the fridge."

Love Consumed

Butterfly touch soft, sensual
Settling on silken skin, words
Unspoken, exploration gentle
Lips brush tenderly as
Bodies entwine, hungrily
Love's heightened plane
Reached as passion consumes
Drifting, floating, rising
Waves of joy, love
Washing over and through
As hearts pound, flesh glistens
Bodies spent
Love consumed

The Bird Club

Gawky, young spindly youths on the cusp of manhood,
insecurity rife

Could have gone either way – fight! fight! fight! – baying for
blood

Chanting in the playground, no shortage of takers, crowds
gathered

Blood spats, broken noses, and never a good outcome

Mr. Few, the Geography teacher, took Ornithology classes after
school

He tried to tempt them in; the wayward boys, the no-hopers,
the loafers

With promises of field trips and a free badge to sport on their
Crombie coats

As if that would lure them in; a field trip – maybe but a badge.
No way.

Binoculars were called 'bins' and educational pamphlets
crumpled in disrespect

The core of the class keen and interested in birds wore their
binoculars with pride

Pencils sharpened and notebooks at the ready, they were a
pleasure to teach

Even the boys at the back quietened, intrigued, happy to be
doing something different

The bird table near the fountain at the main entranceway to the
school building
Was where they all gathered, at a distance, on school benches
hushed by Mr. Few
A tiny goldfinch skittered to the feeder clinging to the side,
pecking the seeds
It's blood-red cap and bright yellow go-faster stripes on its
wings pretty and alluring
Urban landscapes in the concrete jungle of the new town where
the school was built
Offered little scope for wildlife to flourish, save for
handkerchief-sized gardens
Attached to rows and rows of identical plain brick houses,
every front door the same
The residents scratching a living in the post-war era of 1950s
Britain food rationing
Fresh in people's minds, second-hand clothes the norm, home-
made uniforms
A necessity to make ends meet.
"Your boy in that Bird Club, Marge?"
"Yes. Is yours?"
"No! Said it was for sissies. Left school early and got a job.
Brings home a fortune."
Marge unpacked her groceries and stashed them neatly in the
larder

Her two kids, Shirley and Billy, were out in the garden, hiding in some tent they'd made

Eating jam sandwiches and watching birds through their binoculars

The ones they'd had to borrow from school. Pete's wages could never have stretched that far

She'd seen Paul, her friend's son, driving a flashy new car and wondered how he could afford it

None of her business. She had a meal for four to prepare out of a few scraps, but

She was used to it. Pete would get a promotion one day. She was looking for work

Besides, she enjoyed listening to Shirley and Billy discussing birds at the dinner table

Hot Air Balloon

High into the air we float
On our way to where?
To see the world from way up high; we fly

Air rushing into silk
Instantly transporting us upward
Reeling in the beauty of the light

Bound for a magical shore
A blissful haven of retreat
Lullabies of peaceful, mythical times
Luring us into their arms
Of ancient past times ingrained in our hearts
Over, above and far, far away
Nirvana awaits

Double Trouble

The pool party was in full swing by the time Julia arrived. Professor Brooks from Obs and Gynae was being hauled out from the deep end, fully clothed, by some sheepish colleagues. Julia smiled as she breezed past the raised bougainvillea bed; he was usually so debonaire and fastidious about his appearance. She was his PA and although she had only worked for him for a couple of weeks, she was proud to work for such an eminent professor, who was also a really nice guy.

"I'm still wearing my watch, for Chrissakes!" he grumbled in his Australian accent, squelching off towards the host's villa. He was shaking his head and muttering something about his hand-made shoes being ruined.

Julia had only recently arrived from the UK to start a new life as an 'Executive Assistant' at the military hospital in Jeddah and to join her new husband who had been there for over a year. He was being weirdly evasive about the party and told her very matter-of-factly that he would follow on later, after his game of squash with his friend. She was a bit miffed because, being the newbie on the scene, she could have done with some company but undeterred, she crossed the compound alone and found the party easily enough.

"Hey, look at you!" Tammy cooed, giving Julia a big, welcoming hug. They were colleagues at the hospital and had become friends.

"You look gorgeous. What can I get you to drink? You must help yourself to the buffet – there's plenty there. Come and meet some guests."

Julia trailed behind her in her white linen trousers and floaty top. Tammy was a great hostess, but she felt overwhelmed with all the questions and wasn't given the chance to answer any of them. She managed to grab a drink from a tray held out by a passing waiter as Tammy led her alongside the turquoise pool which was under-lit and looked beautiful.

Chuck, Tammy's husband, was holding court with a small group of guests who were sitting around a table at the corner of the pool, telling them how fantastic going out over the edge of the coral reef was at Al-Nakheel beach.

"It's like falling off a cliff but only you're floating! The temperature dips as soon as you go over the edge. It's awesome."

Julia was enthralled and loved the idea of beach outings, barbecues, pool parties, and a ton of other outdoor activities all being pencilled into diaries for the foreseeable. Back in the UK, the summer months run from May (if you're lucky) through to August or possibly September but after that, it gets cold, dark, and very wet. The idea of arranging an outdoor event several weeks ahead was alien to her, but one aspect of working in the Middle East that she was looking forward to more than anything.

Chuck introduced her to the circle of friends, some of whom she had seen at the hospital but not been formally introduced to, and everybody was kind and friendly. They were discussing the merits of various diving courses. Ben had done his PADI diving course, naturally, as soon as he had arrived in the Kingdom, but if Julia was honest, she just wanted to spend her precious one-and-a-half-day weekend on Thursday afternoon and Friday, lazing in the sun and only venturing into the Red Sea to cool off. A short stint of snorkelling would be plenty for her to deal with; she was a sun-seeker and loved the fact that her skin was turning a gorgeous mahogany brown; it made her look glowing and radiant.

"Julia! Come and say hi to some of the guys who work in the Director's Office."

Chuck was a wonderful host and intermingled with his guests like a pro. It was obvious that he was a seasoned ex-pat and Julia thought the Americans were such generous hosts.

Turning to a tall, slender lady wearing an expensive designer dress, he introduced them to each other.

"This is Louise. She's from the UK too." Chuck left them to it to recharge his glass.

"Hi, Louise. Pleased to meet you." Julia went to shake the elegant woman's hand but the older woman took out a packet of cigarettes and lit one up. She inhaled deeply and blew the smoke out upwards, avoiding the young woman opposite her.

"Would you like one?" she asked, huskily.

"No. Thanks. I gave up last year."

"Oh, sorry."

"Don't be."

Secretly, Julia was desperate for a cigarette but she fought the urge.

"How long have you been out here?" she asked, tucking a stray blonde hair behind her ear.

Exhaling another plume of smoke before she spoke, Louise said rather haughtily, "Just over a year. You?"

Julia felt uncomfortable in this woman's company and looked anxiously around for Ben. Where the hell was he?

"Oh, I just got here a couple of weeks ago. It's all still very new."

"Yes, I can tell you're new," she said sardonically. "You look like a rabbit caught in headlights." She looked Julia up and down as she spoke, taking in the pristine new outfit and pretty, delicate sandals.

"Louise! I see you've met Ben's wife, Julia." Professor Brooks had re-joined the party and was now wearing some shorts and a Dubai Creek Golf and Yacht Club polo shirt, courtesy of Chuck, Julia presumed, as it looked a little tight across the chest. He was also wearing flip-flops which looked completely out of character, but he looked calmer and was carrying a plate of food.

"Ben, um?" Louise inquired, waving her cigarette around affectedly.

"Pilkston," Julia replied nonchalantly.

Louise's cigarette stopped mid-way to her mouth and she froze with a horrid look on her face.

"Are you alright, Louise? You look like you've seen a ghost," the professor observed, posting a delicious-looking tiger prawn into his mouth.

"Ben Pilkston, works in Bio-medical Engineering?" she snapped.

"The very one!" Julia piped up proudly. Ben had always been a bit of a ladies' man but Julia had managed to tame him, although he had been very difficult to tie down to a date for the wedding. There was always some problem at the hospital and he couldn't get leave or the visa department was on a go-slow, the excuses were wearing thin. Eventually, though she had managed to become Mrs. Pilkston because if Julia wanted something, Julia got it. They had not long returned from their honeymoon in Mauritius.

"Do you know him?" Julia asked, feeling the upper hand and quite enjoying the moment as she sipped her drink.

"Well, I bloody well should know him. He's my husband!"

Julia didn't feel the champagne flute slip between her fingers, just the cool liquid and the shards of glass across her feet as it smashed on the poolside tiles.

Motherhood

Mouth gaping, the tiny mite reaches out
Nestling into her bosom which aches with love
For this fragrant form that she
Instinctively protects, fiercely
Forsaking all others, barring intruders
A vacuum encircling mother and child
Like a precious bloom, it flourishes
Rich and full, wholesome, complete

Exhaustion is shrugged off like a shroud
Worn stoically with grim monotony
Loving hands guide and protect
An endless source of sustenance, physical and mental
A boiling-pot of remedies, solutions, goals and dreams
Fuelled, stoked and re-stoked, time after time after time
Stirring those dreams into life
Watching them grow and mature into adulthood
With pride, with love

Sunshine and Showers

When at last the sun came out
Peeping intermittently from scudded skies
A child's voice jostled with the woman's thoughts
The heady scent of hibiscus still sweet
Scarlet trumpets blowing through her mind's eye
Oblivious of the old woman by her side
Aware only of the frolicking child dappled in sunshine
Acutely self-conscious of her sagging midriff

In between the hop-skip-and-jump of life
The woman dallied, faded by broken dreams
Knife-edged love for her child bit into her
The man beside her wallowing in her love
A sultry smile in the sea swept scent of life
Oblivious of the old woman by her side
Aware only of the man's tender touch
Acutely aware of the old woman's stare

Glorious Spring

Sunshine yellow trumpets sway rhythmically beneath budding hedgerows
Pops of purple with orange saffron throats stand erect, mouths open
Feeding on mother nature's warm, mossy soil as they drink in the watery sun
As spring bursts into life, splashing vibrant colours across earth's pallid canvas

Chaffinches, blue tits, robins; star-bursts of pretty birds chirrup with joy
At the abundance of berries and seeds, rich pickings from nature's larder
As they busy themselves nesting, preening and feasting, spring-cleaning
Preparing for parenthood; clutches of delicate, speckled eggs incubated

As landscapes erupt from dormant states bursting with life, with hope
Magnolia blossoms candle-like at first, unfurl into exotic, waxy blooms

Cherry blossoms burst into fluffy pink pom-poms of subtle candyfloss hues
Spring lambs bounce, tails wagging as they nudge their mothers' udders

Spring will fade into summer, will fade into autumn, will fade into winter
So the cycle begins again, repeating as the seasons ebb and flow, each one
A unique gift of joy, of life and death, flourishing, wilting and withering
Rejoicing in nature's rich tapestry as she wraps her mantle around us

Reflections

The wise old jeweller scrutinised the sapphire and diamond ring through his loupe eye-glass, twisting it this way and that in between his skilled fingertips. The soft grunting noises he made signalled neither good nor bad news. Mary waited patiently, clutching her shopping bag and shifting impatiently from one foot to another.

The old man behind the counter was examining her engagement ring. Bought in this very shop so many years ago when she and Bob had been young, carefree and head over heels in love. She remembered how eagerly Bob had taken the five- and one-pound notes from his wallet, even though it had meant selling his motorbike, laying them on the counter for Mr. Brooksbank to count. Then, almost in a ceremonial fashion, the assistant had lifted the ring from its royal blue velvet bedding and given it to Bob, who placed it on Mary's finger, there and then.

Mary blushed at the memory and smiled to herself at the way things had turned out between her and Bob. He was a good husband and a doting father to their two boys. She could have done a lot worse.

"I'm afraid I'll have to send it away," the old man declared, taking the eyepiece and putting it to one side. "The claw has been damaged and the work is a little too delicate for my old hands, I'm afraid."

He spoke slowly, his words full of compassion. He could see how much the ring meant to Mary, and he smiled at the memory of the young couple who had betrothed their love to each other all those years ago.

Mary was unsure what to do. If she had the ring repaired and sent away, Bob would notice that she wasn't wearing it. But it was out of the question to wear it as it was. It looked awful; an ugly gaping hole where once sat a beautiful diamond; like graffiti on a work of art, a blot an all those happy years. There was nothing else for it; she would have to tell Bob.

She thanked the man for his time and placed the ring into a small black box which he had given her. Tucking it safely into her handbag, she walked slowly through the shopping precinct, stopping now and again to browse at the brightly lit windows displaying new summer fashions and footwear. It was in the reflection of one such window that she saw Bob. He was reading a magazine and seemed to be hanging around as if waiting for someone. Then she saw Jean, their next-door neighbour, and close friend. They were both laughing and seemed quite triumphant, almost celebratory. They linked arms and, still smiling broadly, made for a nearby coffee shop.

Bob had been acting strangely of late, side-stepping questions of his whereabouts, and he had been putting in a lot of overtime recently. Sometimes four or five evenings a week, not the odd one or two. Mary made for a concourse of wooden seats amidst an avalanche of greenery and sat down. Tucking herself away in a corner, trying to be invisible, she

buried herself in her thoughts.

Had she been that neglectful? She admitted not having as much time for Bob as she perhaps had in the early days of their marriage, but the boys still demanded a lot of her time, dumping great bag loads of washing on her at weekends, Ian from his bedsit and Michael from his digs at college. And she had taken a part-time job at the local hospice which recently had somehow extended almost into full-time. But the money was handy. The boys always seemed to need something and their rents weren't cheap either. Now, having seen Bob and Jean together looking so happy, she wondered sadly whether it had all been worth it.

Catching the next bus home, she tried to forget what she had just seen. Trying to convince herself that it was probably completely innocent, she set about the household chores with a slow hand. She almost missed the wad of notes tucked away at the back of Bob's bedside cabinet drawer, they were so well concealed in an old sock. Flicking through the notes quickly, she counted almost eight hundred pounds. Replacing them exactly where she had found them, she felt physically sick.

"Mary! I'm home, love! Had a good day?" She could hear Bob down in the kitchen and she stopped to tidy herself in the mirror. She was still an attractive woman and had kept herself in good shape. Her hair was beautifully styled but was showing silvery flecks of grey, but she liked the distinguished look it gave her. Rubbing some rouge into her pale cheeks and painting her full lips with a soft peach lipstick, she suddenly felt a lot better about her appearance. She even saw a flicker of a sparkle return to her wise eyes. There was a lot of life left in her yet and she was going to enjoy it. With or without Bob. She chided herself for thinking such thoughts. Of course, Bob wouldn't leave her, would he? 'Till death us do part.' That's what they had said, all those years ago. 'Till death us do part.'

She went down to greet her husband, but instead of pecking him casually on the cheek as she usually did, she brushed straight past him and busied herself at the sink.

"What's wrong, love. Are you okay?"

Slowly, she poured two coffees, surreptitiously wiping a tear from her eye.

"Bob. I've got something to tell you. My engagement ring. I've lost one of the stones out of it and it's damaged. It must have happened while I was gardening."

From behind his newspaper, Bob responded, "Don't worry, love. I'll get it fixed."

Suddenly, the tears welled up and overflowed. Why had she been so foolish? Letting those years slip away, not showing him how much she cared. Letting domesticity creep into their lives, choking them with its boredom and routine.

"Hey, love. What's the matter?" Bob put his paper down and held her to him in a warm embrace. She wanted to push him away.

"I saw you today. With Jean," she blurted out. The words sounded choked and strangled in between her sobs.

"Oh, Mary. I should have told you. I'm so sorry." Releasing her, he reached for his jacket on the back of the kitchen chair. He was still a handsome man, broad-shouldered and lean. Mary still got butterflies sometimes when she looked at him.

"I've booked a surprise for you," he said, showing her a brochure.

Mary looked up, wiping her eyes. "But we've just come back from holiday," she said, confused.

"That was different. This is just you and me. I've got tickets for the Orient Express. Don't tell me you've forgotten? It's our silver wedding anniversary next month and Jean has been helping me to arrange it all. She said you had been telling her how much you would love to go."

Mary stopped crying.

"All that overtime," Bob continued, "was to help pay for the trip and I've still got some left over to buy you an eternity ring. We never did get round to buying you one, did we?"

"Oh, Bob! How could I have even thought such a thing?" She felt stupid for doubting the man that she loved as much today, if not more, than she had when they first got engaged all those years ago.

"Before we go, though," Bob said, 'we'll pay a visit to Brooksbank's and get that ring repaired. And, being as you've spoiled my surprise, you can choose your own eternity ring. I probably wouldn't have chosen one you liked anyway."

Baking Day

Cross-legged and furrow-browed
Egg-shells cave on impact
Slimy deposits cling to little fingers
A grimace distorts her pretty face

Discarding shells, she takes up a whisk
Ingredients combine into a lumpy paste
"What colour eyes does God have, Mum?"
The woman turns, caught off guard

"I don't know, darling. What do you think?"
A triumphant smile follows a frown. "Blue!"
Skits of goo shower the worktop
"All babies are born with blue eyes."

Cookbook abandoned, the woman stops
"And that's God's soul in the baby."
As quickly as the subject came, it left
"Can I put this in the tin?"

Pots, pans, tins and tools
Litter the small kitchen. The sink
Awash with sticky messes, soaking
In bubbles that have long since burst

The child licks her sticky fingers
"Why do you look so sad?"
A smile, designed to reassure, crosses the woman's face
"I'm not sad, darling. Just thinking."

A Chance Encounter

"Ice-cold towel, madam?"

Melinda raised her head from the sun lounger and peered at the young man proffering her a bowl piled with white flannels soaked in ice-cold water.

"Thank you," she said, taking one from the top and removing her sunglasses before settling it on her face, grateful for the coolness against her hot skin. The temperature today was 40° F – normal for this time of year – and laying by the pool on the weekend was all Melinda was fit for after working ten-hour days all week at the American law firm where she worked as a Legal Assistant.

As the cool flannel began to warm in the intense heat, she removed it, and there he was again, the super-efficient pool attendant but this time, he was offering a tray of assorted sliced melon with cotton napkins. She took one slice, with a crisp white napkin and he efficiently removed the used face towel with a bow of his head and a beautiful smile, backing discreetly away, leaving Melinda with her thoughts on another day in the opulent metropolis that was her home.

The Address Downtown hotel was actually her home; she rented a suite on the twelfth floor which she could only afford since the financial crash of 2008. She had been living in shared accommodation at Marsa Plaza, another imposing modern building overlooking Dubai Creek, but sharing with three guys wasn't ideal. They each had their own rooms and en suite bathrooms but late-night gatherings in the lounge next to her room kept her awake into the small hours so, when she woke up one morning in February 2009 to see no cranes moving on the horizon as she stood at the floor-to-ceiling glass windows of her shared apartment, she knew something was seriously wrong. The stillness was eerie; no worker ants scurrying around in the desert heat, no movement at all save for cars glinting in the distance as they snaked their way along the Persian Gulf state's roads. That was three months ago.

Working in a law firm had been fortunate for her due to the nature of their work, but thousands of expats had been forced to flee the Emirate after their jobs had simply disappeared, dumping their cars at the airport before they left. Melinda was glad she had decided not to buy a car but instead used taxis to travel back and forth to work. A good move in hindsight; if a debt is not paid in Dubai, foreigners can be sent to debtor's prison.

With so many people having lost their jobs she was grateful that hers was safe; in fact, she had been asked by the Office Manager to work extra hours if she was able to but she had declined; a 48-hour week was quite long enough for her.

As Melinda made her way to the Zeta bar for a refreshing drink and a light lunch, she walked briskly to the elevator to take her down the three floors, which was preferable to walking in the intense summer heat, which was stifling and almost unbearable.

As the elevator slipped elegantly into position and the doors opened, she was conscious of somebody running behind her.

"Hold the elevator, please," she heard, and as she stepped inside, pressed the 'door hold' button.

"Thank you," a man with olive skin and a very seductive voice said, as he stepped inside the capsule next to her. "Which floor would you like?" he asked, his elegant hand hovering over the numerous buttons.

"Three, please," Melinda responded, clutching her pool-side bag and feeling slightly dishevelled after her morning's sunbathing.

"Ah, me too. I'm heading to the Zeta bar for lunch. Would you care to join me?"

Melinda was taken aback but there was something very attractive about the man's personality, as well as his suave, chiselled features which she thought may have Omani origins. Living in Dubai, she met such a cross-section of people from so many different nationalities, she was quite good at guessing where people were from.

"Um, well, perhaps we could have a drink, but I need to get back as I'm meeting friends a little later," she lied.

"Okay," he said, sounding disappointed. "A drink it is, then."

The perfect gentleman, he stepped to one side as the elevator's doors slid apart and she stepped out onto the terrace of the bar. As a single woman living alone in Dubai, she was all too aware of the dangers of meeting strangers and was careful not to let too much slip about where she lived.

"Are you visiting Dubai or do you live here?" her companion asked.

"I live here. I work at an American law firm."

"Ah. Interesting. My name is Adnan, by the way. You are?"

"Melinda, pleased to meet you," she responded, stretching out her small hand. He had a firm but gentle handshake and a frisson of excitement shot through her and she smiled at the handsome man who had already caught the eye of a waiter and was speaking perfect English. The waiter led the way to a table shaded by an enormous beige parasol so it was completely in the shade.

"I think perhaps we should arrange to have dinner another time because very disappointingly, you have other plans for later today." His smile was mischievous yet alluring and he had a wonderful depth to his eyes. He looked wise and intelligent and sophisticated and Melinda's stomach was doing somersaults. She wished she would have checked her appearance in a mirror before leaving the pool area and surreptitiously fluffed up her blonde hair, hoping it didn't look too unruly. At age 34, she knew that her make-up-free face, which was tanned and glowing, wasn't too bad but again, she wished she had made more of an effort.

"What do you do, Adnan?" she enquired as the waiter promptly brought their drinks and discreetly set a glass of sparkling water in front of each of them.

"I am a businessman here on business but unfortunately, I leave tomorrow." He made a sad face, and Melinda smiled.

"Are you sure I can't tempt you to delay seeing your friends and accompany me to dinner this evening?"

Melinda thought it couldn't do any harm, especially as he was leaving tomorrow, so she agreed.

"Fantastic! I will send a driver to collect you at 7 pm, if that's OK for you?"

Melinda nodded, trying not to be too enthusiastic.

"Yes, seven o'clock is fine." She smiled warmly at the man opposite her.

"That's settled then." With that, Adnan caught the waiter's eye, whispered something in his ear, and before Melinda knew it, he had gone, saying how much he looked forward to seeing her later.

As she made her way back up to her suite, Melinda wondered whether she had just dreamt the chance encounter with the handsome Omani man; perhaps the heat was playing tricks with her mind.

A refreshing shower and an afternoon nap cleared her head and checking her watch for the umpteenth time, she made her way down to Reception, wishing she had had the foresight to get Adnan's mobile number because she was wondering whether to decline his invitation. After all, she knew nothing about him. What did 'businessman' mean exactly? He could be in any sort of business from dealing drugs (which was highly improbable) to selling fake art (also very unlikely).

Dressed in an elegant black cocktail dress with shoestring straps, she had piled her hair into a chignon and made a special effort with her make-up. Her eyes were sparkling at the prospect of seeing Adnan again but she suddenly realised that she didn't even know his driver's name. Clutching her delicate beaded handbag, she looked around the huge marble foyer which was full of Western and Arab guests out for the evening; the Address Downtown Dubai was a popular destination with its stunning array of award-winning restaurants ranging from the Cigar Lounge for light bites to The Garden, which overlooked the Burj Khalifa and Souk Al Bahar.

"Miss Melinda?" a young Indian man enquired, having just spoken to a waiter.

"Yes. Are you Adnan's driver?"

"I am, madam. My car is outside; Adnan has asked me to take you to him."

Suddenly, Melinda felt incredibly nervous. Why wasn't Adnan in the car? Where would this young stranger take her?

Sensing her discomfort, the young chauffeur introduced himself. "My name is Rahul, madam, and Mr. Adnan was called to an urgent meeting and sends his apologies."

Melinda's heart sank. Was her date off? She hesitated as she stood next to the black limousine where Rahul was waiting with the door open.

"Is Adnan coming this evening?" she asked tentatively, standing her ground firmly with no intention of getting into the back seat of the imposing car.

"Of course, madam. He apologised because he was not able to come in person to collect you. He is waiting for you."

With a slight hesitation, Melinda decided to get into the back of a complete stranger's car driven by somebody she had only just met. As they pulled away from the hotel forecourt very slowly due to the heavy traffic of people being disgorged and milling around and others waiting for taxis who were queueing up the driveway, she pulled out her mobile phone and dialled her friend, Angelique, an Indian lady she worked with and was here in Dubai with her husband, Rohit.

"Hi, Angelique. How are you?" she inquired when her friend answered after the second ring.

"I'm okay; how about you? Is everything okay?"

"Yes, I'm just being driven to meet Adnan, a man I met at the Address Downtown today and he invited me for dinner."

"Wow! Lucky girl. You have a date, at long last," she teased.

Slightly embarrassed that the driver could hear her conversation, but that was the whole point of the call, she said, "I don't know where I'm going but I'll let you know as soon as I arrive."

Angelique immediately picked up on what her friend was asking her to do.

"Of course. Please keep me informed," she replied with a serious tone in her voice.

Melinda ended the call and was slightly perturbed when the driver took the road to the airport.

"Rahul, where are we going?" she asked, trying to keep the hysteria out of her voice.

"A surprise, madam. Adnan asked me not to tell you. He loves surprises. Do you, madam?"

"Well, that all depends on whether it's a nice surprise or a nasty one," she replied sarcastically.

"Don't worry, madam. You will have a wonderful evening, I am certain," he said in his sing-song Indian accent.

The car pulled up next to a helicopter with a pilot waiting and before she knew what was happening, Rahul had opened the car door and was offering his hand to help her out. Her high heels were hardly conducive to a helicopter ride and she felt rather foolish for dressing up so smartly.

"Good evening, madam," the pilot greeted her, "This way please."

Taken aback by the speed with which everything had happened, the next thing Melinda knew was that she was hovering over the city of Dubai and headed out to sea. Her stomach was in knots but she couldn't help but enjoy the ride; the view was spectacular and the city in the desert sparkled in the shimmering dusk light beneath her.

Suddenly, the pilot's voice cut into her thoughts. "Our destination is just ahead of us, ma'am. The Burj Al Arab – Adnan is waiting for you in the Skyview bar."

Melinda took in the amazing Palm Island just beyond the magnificent sail-shaped Burj Al-Arab, which was situated at the end of a long causeway out in the azure blue sea; it was as beautiful as it was iconic.

As the helicopter approached, she spotted a tiny white car pulling up at the main entrance of the hotel, which was sitting on a triangular plot in the Arabian Gulf. It was almost surreal in its beauty and opulence and as they rounded the back of the hotel, she spotted the sleek Skyview bar which looked like a small, white cylindrical mouth organ stuck to the side of the hotel on the 27th floor.

As they approached the circular landing pad, which looked tiny from where they were, Melinda felt a mixture of fear and excitement, and she waited patiently as the pilot skilfully navigated his way onto the helipad on the opposite side to the bar. The engine quietened from a high-pitched whine to a slower, mechanical sound and she saw a man waiting on the steps, his grey suit billowing in the strong downdraught from the helicopter. He had the biggest grin and was waving furiously.

"I have delivered you safely to your Prince Charming, ma'am. Have a wonderful evening."

"Thank you so much!" she enthused.

Adnan was walking towards her and in all the excitement, she had clean forgotten to ring Angelique back to tell her where she was.

"Melinda! I am so sorry I could not come to the hotel to accompany you here with Rahul but my meeting has only just finished. Do you forgive me?" he asked, helping her out of the helicopter and holding her to him. His expensive cologne tantalised her and she resisted kissing him there and then, in front of the pilot.

As they walked hand-in-hand down the steps from the helipad and into the hotel, Melinda felt an excitement that she hadn't felt in such a long time. This was one hell of a first date.

Do Not Hurt Me, I am Too Weak

Do not hurt me, I am too weak
My captor's vengeance sickly and vile
Smashed by your heartless fist beating my soul

Robotic days turn into restless nights
Suffocation seeps through my soul
Do not hurt me, I am too weak

Anger, rage, and bloody torment
Fight against the blinding light
Smashed by your heartless fist beating my soul

Callous, spiteful hurt inflicted daily
My mummified shell once full and voluptuous
Do not hurt me, I am too weak

Slay me and be done with all the suffering
Or let me free to escape your bloodied hands
Smashed by your heartless fist beating my soul

Time seeps out and drains away, contaminated
By your grasp upon my passion for life
Do not hurt me, I am too weak
Smashed by your heartless fist beating my soul.

Peace of Mind

Jagged, sharp and wretched
Spiky from life's insatiable demands
Frustrations build like a volcano
Belly-deep howls break free
Why? Why? Why me?

Let me flap and flounder
On life's shores of wisdom
Saluting the genius of youth
Gliding through life
As we once knew it

Technophobes unite, angry
Why? Why? Why me?
Let me be; please, free me
From the mysteries I face
Which threaten to engulf me

Why can't life be easier?
Free-wheeling, happy, innocent
Care-free days of our youth
Honesty, clarity, vision
Simplicity and peace of mind

It's all I ask. Before I die.

The Summer of 1974

Mom has another new boyfriend.

It seems that since Dad left she's never been happy. Sometimes I go outside and wander the neighborhood for something to do. I don't think she misses me. My older sister, Cal, is away traveling the world. I always envied Cal. She seems to know where she's going in life. A free spirit, not a care in the world. I miss her.

I'll never forget the day she left. One minute she was stuffing her rucksack with yet one more pair of hotpants that she couldn't possibly live without or a tiny teensy cheesecloth shirt, so happy and excited. Like she had her whole life ahead of her. Which she did, I guess. I was the young, gangly teenager with spots and buck teeth. Cal was the tanned, athletic, beautiful even-teeth all-American smile kinda gal.

I don't know what happened that day, but Mom got mad because she had planned a special meal because Jed was moving in with us. He was gonna be our new 'dad'. I didn't like Jed. I don't know why but he just creeped me out. Anyhow, Cal must have said something because the next thing, she's running off down the sidewalk to catch the Greyhound bus without even looking back at me. She never said goodbye. I was heartbroken.

Mom said Cal was selfish and never had bothered with her younger sister but that's not true. We used to be close when Dad lived with us. We played out back together and dressed up in pretty homemade things we had picked out of each other's wardrobes. Cal even did my make-up once. But that was all before Dad left. Everything changed after he left.

I often cry when I read the last postcard I ever got from my big sister. She was on her way to New Zealand, she said. But she never made it.

"I'll come back for you as soon as I can, Sissy. Keep strong and don't take any shit from Mom."

I never knew what she meant because Mom had always been okay with me; not a good mom but not a bad one either. I had clean clothes, food on the table and I paid my dues by helping round the house. That's how it always was.

It was only when Mom told me that Cal had been involved in a hit-and-run accident on her way to the airport somewhere in Europe, that I realized I would never see her again. I was heartbroken.

'What you don't know can't hurt you' is a saying that I can live by. For over fifty years, I thought Cal had been killed in a hit-and-run accident. I never questioned Mom about the where, why, and how. I just wasn't the inquisitive type. It was only after Mom died that I found a shoebox full of letters and mementos that Cal and I had given her as kids. Buried deep down inside the old cardboard box was a letter that Cal must have sent her from Europe. I cried and cried when I read it.

Suddenly, the words on the postcard that she had sent me made a little bit more sense.

"I hate you, Mom, for turning a blind eye to all those guys you brought home with me and Sissy in the house. I was seventeen but Sissy was just a kid... how could you? You were always weak. I will never forgive you. I have an appointment tomorrow to have an abortion. It's Jed's. I hope you kick that no-good son-of-a-bitch out and pay more attention to Sissy. She deserves way more than you could ever give her."

I held the letter close to my heart. So that's how my sister had died. Mom had lied to me and never told me the truth. But she had had to live with that torment for the rest of her life.

Jed didn't last long, I remember because after Cal left so suddenly, Mom kicked him out and it was just me and her after that.

I wish Cal had talked to me. But, as she said, I was just a kid.

Unconditional Love

Tiny arms cling to my neck
Soft skin and perfect teeth
Gleaming eyes wide, bright alert
Love has no bounds
Innocence of love, unconditional
Precious moments in time
Cling to my heart, melting it
Every time those arms wrap around me
Enveloping me in sweetness and love
Mesmerising as time stands still
How I wish I could freeze time
And stay in this moment forever
To enjoy this carefree time together
When love has no bounds

Cursed

The arid, dusty floor of the tomb was soft beneath Laura's canvas shoes.

After crawling through the tight passageway to the burial chamber and standing upright, she was surprised at how small the chamber was. She compared it to the size of her bedroom in their small, terraced house in London. All that was in the chamber was a stone sarcophagus.

"Wow! Mum, isn't this fantastic?" her twelve-year-old gushed. Suki was studying Egyptology at school and had always wanted to visit the pyramids.

"Yes," Laura responded dreamily, her head tilted back as she took in every aspect of the chamber. It felt eerie to be alone inside the pyramid with just Suki for company. And the sarcophagus. As if drawn to it like a magnet, the two of them wondered if it would be alright to touch the sacred tomb.

Suki's face suddenly clouded over.

"Mum! Don't!" she demanded in a very serious voice. "You know what happened to Howard Carter."

"Oh, that's just…"

"What?" Suki probed, raising her eyebrows and giving her mother a challenging look. "It's a fact that he died soon after opening Tutankhamen's tomb."

"He contracted blood poisoning, which he could have caught anywhere," Laura retorted.

"Well, in school we all think he died because he disturbed the Pharaoh's tomb. So, please don't touch the sarcophagus."

Laura knew better than to defy her daughter. Besides, she didn't want to tempt fate.

They both stood for a few minutes, taking in the enormity of where they were, revelling in the fact that they had finally achieved their dream. They had not only visited the pyramids but they were actually standing inside one. It was Laura who eventually broke the spell.

"Come on. We'd better go and find Dad."

Suki smiled at the mention of her dad. "I wonder if he's still on that camel or whether he fell off!"

"Don't say that! He could hurt himself and I don't fancy wasting our holiday waiting around in an Egyptian hospital."

Right on cue their young guide, Hassan, appeared at the entrance of the tomb.

"Ready, ma'am?" he asked, a cheeky grin on his face. He sauntered over to the sarcophagus and before Laura or Suki could stop him, he hopped on top and pulled a half-smoked cigarette from his kaftan pocket. Swinging his sandalled feet up on to the tomb, he pulled out a lighter and lit up.

"You can't smoke in here!" Suki admonished. "And I don't think you should be sitting on the sarcophagus either!"

Her voice was high-pitched and taut. She stood close to her mother as if seeking reassurance.

"She's right, Hassan. I don't think it's very respectful. We'd better go. Come on."

"Okey-dokey," he quipped, mimicking an English saying he had heard from the tourists. He snuffed out the cigarette butt with his fingers and stuffed it back into his pocket.

A few minutes later, after inching their way awkwardly back down the tight passageway with wooden strips embedded into it, they emerged into the blistering heat and scrambled in their bags to find their sunglasses. Laura checked that Suki was wearing her sunhat and looked at her watch. They had agreed to meet David back here, but he was nowhere to be seen.

A throng of Arabs and tourists mingled in the desert surrounding the pyramids; the heat was almost unbearable. Laura realised why the Arabs wore long, flowing cotton thobes and ghutras to shade their head and neck. She passed a water bottle from her bag to Suki and watched as she drank thirstily before passing it back.

"There he is!" Suki yelled excitedly.

A wave of relief washed over Laura as she saw David waving in the distance, striding towards them. He was wearing chinos and a long-sleeved blue linen shirt. He was carrying his straw fedora hat and reaching into his pocket.

"What do you fancy doing now, Suki?" Laura asked.

The youngster drew a picture in the sand with her foot.

"What's that?"

Suki smiled up at her mother.

"Ah. I'm supposed to understand hieroglyphics now, am I?" They both laughed.

"Did you enjoy the tomb?" David asked, wiping his brow with a handkerchief and smiling broadly. "Let's get out of this damned heat. I'm melting. You can tell me all about it later."

The three of them marched off, Indian file towards the road and as they hurried along, David was hailing a taxi. Miraculously, a beaten up, dirty old Mercedes pulled up at the kerbside to greet them.

"Mena House Hotel," David instructed. "Shukraan." He sat in the front to make sure the driver didn't take the long route. Laura and Suki clambered into the back seat.

The air-conditioning in the cab was icy cool and a revelation to the appearance of the car from the outside. The relief from the stifling heat was most welcome and Laura would have paid the driver double for the luxury of the cool interior. She sat back and closed her eyes as the car sped along.

Suddenly, the taxi screeched to a halt and a camel with a young boy on the back plodded across the road. The driver bellowed something in Arabic out through the window before quickly drawing it back up again to stop the heat pervading the cool interior. The boy shouted something back and gesticulated, but they couldn't hear him.

"Mum. Wasn't that Hassan?" Suki asked.

By the time Laura opened her eyes, the boy had disappeared among a crowd of tourists.

As the cab drew up outside the hotel, David handed the driver the fare with a generous tip.

"Shukraan, Habibi."[1]

"Shukraan jazilaan."[2] the driver responded, smiling as he drove away.

The bell-boy at the hotel entrance greeted the family like long lost friends, even though they had only been at the hotel for a couple of days.

"Good afternoon, sir. Very hot, today, sir. Very hot." The young man was dressed immaculately in black pantaloons, a white blouson shirt and a purple waistcoat with a matching bell-boy hat. He had the most beautiful smile and he opened the door quickly and gracefully, ushering his guests inside to the marble foyer, with its imposing pillars and impressive views across to the pyramids at Giza.

"Would you like a drink, girls?" David asked, not waiting for them to answer but instead striding off towards the bar. Laura and Suki followed behind.

"One watermelon juice, a pint of Stella and…" He turned to Laura.

"Oh, I'll have a half of Stella, please."

David didn't need to repeat his wife's order. The barman had heard and nodded in acknowledgement; the staff were first-class.

"Take a seat, please, sir, ma'am. I will bring it to your table."

---

[1] Thank you, my friend
[2] Thank you very much

Suki chose the colourful majlis-style sofas nearest to the bar and her parents sank gratefully into the soft cushions.

Mustafa bought the drinks over almost immediately and proceeded to set them out on the brass oval table in front of them, remembering which drink was for whom.

"Did you enjoy your trip today?" he asked.

Suki beamed and told him all about the tomb with the sarcophagus and how she and her mum had climbed up the narrow passageway, which they didn't realise would be so small and the reason why her dad had decided not to go with them, because he thought he might get stuck.

Mustafa smiled warmly at the young girl. "So, you visited the Great Pyramid?"

"Yes!" Suki said, her dark eyes gleaming. "It was amazing!"

"I hope you didn't touch the sarcophagus. It is sacred," he said, his face clouding over.

"No, of course not," Laura interjected.

The waiter bowed politely before returning to his duties at the bar.

Laura made a funny face at Suki, who understood and sipped her juice obediently.

Suddenly, there was a commotion at the entrance to the hotel. A Western man was being helped in by two of the staff. He looked as though he were in shock.

Laura tried to shield Suki from the drama but she managed to peek under her mother's arm.

"It's probably sunstroke," Laura said, gently pulling Suki around to stop her gawping at the man.

They finished their drinks and made their way across to the elevators, avoiding the fracas in the foyer. As they were waiting for the elevator to arrive, David told Laura to go up to their room.

"I'm going to Reception to make sure our booking for the Felucca trip tomorrow is all okay."

Laura smiled at him; she loved the way he organised everything so beautifully. It was probably the reason why all of their holidays ran so smoothly and they always had such a fantastic time. He was such a lovely dad and husband.

Back in their suite, Laura sent Suki to take a shower to cool off and said she would follow. As she waited for her daughter in the lounge area, she sat on the couch admiring the fantastic view across to the pyramids and thought how beautiful and they were.

David arrived a few minutes later looking very concerned.

"What's wrong?" Laura asked, getting up to greet up.

"Did you go into that tomb today? The one in the Great Pyramid with the sarcophagus in it?" he demanded.

Laura blew out her cheeks. "Well, we did go into the tomb but we didn't touch the sarcophagus, if that's what you're asking. Why?"

"It doesn't matter."

"David? What is it?" she asked, her voice full of concern.

"Well, the man they carried in just now was driving a car and he hit a camel. The young boy on the camel was killed. The staff were all shocked and said he was a bit of a character and was well-liked by all the tourists. His name was Hassan."

The colour drained from Laura's face and she felt her knees buckle beneath her.

Memories

Faded days of youth flicker like a silent movie
Memories weakened from replays, over and over
Sanguine, happy times – wild swimming
Horse riding, building camps, climbing trees
Grazed knees dismissed as hunger beckoned

Re-capturing magnificent glory days of warmth
Love discovered for the first time, sweet
Star-bursts of excitement; the scent of cornfields
Haybarns mystical and stirring in their daring
Innocent, happy times – haymaking on the farm

Red-hot poker pain as horseplay ends badly
Riding days over briefly, adolescence beckons
Time to knuckle down, get serious, study hard
The pulley-rope of life hauls me up and over
Into adulthood, jolting me into responsibility

A life that follows me into the horizon
Of my dreams hankering after…after what?
Sodden tears of insipidness threaten to engulf me
With a lacklustre future devoid of excitement
Mundane responsibility falls heavy upon me

Parenthood enriches acres of dreams and beyond
Outstretched and seemingly endless days of love
Beckon on dark days of meagre earnings, the
Dust mites of dreams broken edge closer as
Life hurtles along at break-neck speed. Stop!

Wait for the passenger to alight the
Speeding wagon of sherbet-dab fun-fair candyfloss
Spinning into the vortex of life, haphazard
Lucky dip assortment brought their way
Memories, happy times – keep them safe

The Woman in Black

In the searing desert heat and cloying humidity of a July day in Jeddah, Princess Amaal refused to walk the few steps to the waiting, air-conditioned Lexus. Instead, she made her driver reverse into the triple garage, close the door and wait for her. When she deigned to appear, Younis, wearing a white thobe and ghutra, leapt out from behind the wheel and quickly opened the back door of the car and clicked it shut as soon as she was inside. She was covered from head to toe in black, apart from the gold braid, which trimmed her expensive abeya and hijab. The blacked-out windows prevented anybody from seeing inside the car.

The Princess was one of the lucky ones. Her husband, Prince Jameel, was a wonderful man. He trusted her implicitly and adored her; a good combination. Today, she was going to test that love. She had arranged for their London house in Kensington to be opened up for the summer, where she intended to stay for several weeks. The blistering heat of the desert city was oppressive and a sojourn in England was just what she needed.

Prince Jameel's other three wives had borne him five sons between them, but Amaal had only produced a daughter. She was flying to London to visit one of the world's leading gynaecologists to see if she could assist her in producing a son. Friends of hers had done the same thing and been successful. It was worth a try.

Younis drove sedately along Prince Majid Road towards the King Abdulaziz International Airport and swung the Lexus into a small, unmarked side road and out to the hangar where Prince Jameel's private jet was waiting. He had radioed ahead with his ETA, ensuring that the Princess could board the jet as quickly as possible. Her extensive range of luggage had been loaded the evening before when Younis had done the airport run under the cover of darkness; the nights were so much cooler than the searing daytime heat of summers in the bride of the Red Sea.

As she ascended the steps of the jet in her dainty Jimmy Choo shoes, Princess Amaal was shocked to find her husband already on board. He spoke to her softly in Arabic.

"My dear Amaal. Sit down."

The Princess removed her abeya and hijab once the staff had left them alone, settling her slender figure into one of the enormous plush leather seats opposite her husband. He was incredibly handsome, kind and inspirational. She felt honoured to be one of his wives.

"You must not fret about producing a son. Our beautiful daughter, Enaam, is enough. I don't want you visiting clinics and wasting your time in London when you could be relaxing."

"How did you find out?" she asked, blushing.

"Sweetie. You know that I only have your best interests at heart. I don't need another son. Besides, I rather think Enaam enjoys all the attention from her brothers."

Amaal knew that nothing got past her husband and she ignored the way he had side-stepped her question. She sipped the sparkling water that had been placed on the chic walnut side table next to her. There was a slice of fresh lime and a sprig of mint in it, just the way she liked it.

She reflected for a moment and then smiled at her husband sitting across from her. She could smell his Oud and butterflies started to flit around her insides. She was lucky to have him in her life; things could have turned out very differently.

The Prince continued in his soft, cultured voice, "I have arranged for Enaam to join us in a few days but in the meantime, I am going to accompany you to London. Just until she arrives and then…you two can spend the whole summer there. You can find out what interests her because one day, she will need to choose what she would like to do. Become a doctor perhaps, or even a gynaecologist…" His eyes glittered as he spoke.

A broad smile spread across Amaal's beautiful face. The thought of her daughter studying for a university degree and becoming an eminent doctor or even a surgeon in her chosen field filled her with joy. It was something she had always wanted to do but was never given the opportunity.

As she was about to settle down into her seat for the long flight ahead, her husband handed her a large white box. There, nestled on white velveteen was a replica of the necklace from The Titanic. She gasped when she touched the exquisite heart-shaped sapphire and diamonds looped onto a platinum chain.

She carefully lifted it from the box and draped it around her swan-like neck for her husband to admire.

"Jameel, you spoil me," she said sweetly, happy with the extravagant gift.

The Prince cocked his head slightly to one side.

"You are my Princess. Of course, I will spoil you."

Release Me

Sun-jewelled bespeckled droplets dance on mirrored light
Dappled shafts of rainbow-arced symmetries of life
Nested on the moss-covered cliff tops of wayward walks
Wheeling petrels storm through my mind, squawking, razor-
billed
Piercing, knife-edged pain sears into my soul melting my mind
Threatening to swipe the earth from beneath me, paralysing
The mortality that I feel endlessly shimmering in the candlelight
The focus of my mind edging closer to the drop; plummeting
Blindly, the tattooed weal on my heart, the rhythm of life
Beating like a drum, hum-drumming on my brain, stop
Let me breathe, take my hand, lead me away from the abyss
That I have let you draw me into, vortexed into obscurity
Baying for blood, not content until you suck my gizzards out
Sheep's eyes pecked clean, the socket wide and gaping
Like the hole in my heart that you ripped apart with your smile
Evil in its intention washing over me, draining my life away
Sucking the world away from me as you drawl and salivate
At my misfortune as you mould me into putty, pliable and soft
In your expert grasp, choking me. Please, let me free
And like a butterfly, let me flutter into the breeze and fly away

Daybreak

Sunshine-dappled lawns dance on lighted morns
Glowing in effervescent bursts of colour and beauty
Dawn-chorused cacophonies herald the start
Of a brand-new day; rejoice from the rafters at
Mother Nature's mantle cast across our garden
A network of quilted designs exquisitely formed
Enriching our lives through sight, sound and smell
Evocative, perfunctory and mystical they lay claim
To a myriad of starburst feelings in our hearts
We thank her for enriching our lives so bountifully

Watching Over Us

All those assembled around the oval-shaped boardroom table seemed particularly restless.

The Chairman of the meeting, David Brooks, well-spoken and self-assured, obviously knew how to conduct a meeting and corralled the unruly bunch of people before him into order.

"Ladies and gentlemen," he said authoritatively, tapping a sheaf of papers in front of him on the table neatly aligning them, "let us begin. Cordelia, as Andrew's mother, who do you think would be best suited for him?"

The petite, elderly lady was immaculately turned out in a beautiful emerald-green dress with matching pearls and earrings. "Well, I've seen how Julia and Deborah have conducted themselves and," she paused, looking around the table, "I'm assuming we are down to just two candidates, now?"

A soft murmur rippled around the table and nods headed in agreement. She continued assertively, "In that case, I propose that Deborah be the one."

A woman of a similar age sitting opposite Cordelia smiled and said, "I think that's a good choice."

Cordelia smiled at her and nodded, knowingly.

"So, let's take a vote," David said, clearing his throat. "A show of hands for Julia."

Nobody raised their hand.

"A show of hands for Deborah."

Everybody around the table raised their hands.

"Unanimously carried. A resounding 'yes' for Deborah it is!"

Back down to earth with a bang after her divorce, Deborah had started dating again but hadn't had much luck. In her mid-fifties, she was finding the dating scene extremely difficult to handle after the breakup of her thirty-year marriage. It was like being a teenager again but with all the extra baggage that a lifetime of being married brings – children, a slightly sagging midriff and a heavy heart.

Two hundred miles away across the border in England, Andrew was slowly emerging from his bout of depression following his divorce. Living in a rented barn, which had become known by his close friends as 'the sad barn', he dragged himself off to work and wasn't looking forward to the Friday-night bash that his friends had invited him to in Wales, but he knew they were just trying to help and liked to keep an eye on him. Besides, he had nothing else to do. Julia had told him in no uncertain terms that she'd had enough of his moping about and had ended their short-term relationship with a very curt text. That was all he needed. He liked her and thought the relationship could have gone further. She obviously felt very differently.

When John and Bridget, Deborah's pals from way back when, invited her to their house-warming party that evening, she really wasn't in the mood, but she had nothing else planned other than to binge watch a box set on TV with a glass of wine and a tub of ice-cream for company. Reluctantly, after a long

day at the office, she motivated herself to get dolled up because she knew if she didn't make an effort, Bridget would berate her.

"Do it for yourself, if nothing else. You can't let yourself go just because you're divorced. You're an attractive woman."

Deborah had been to John and Bridget's parties before and they always made an effort, decorating their home beautifully for the occasion and performing as perfect hosts, immaculately turned out themselves.

Andrew arrived bearing gifts of flowers and a bottle of wine which Bridget relieved him of at their front door before ushering him through to the garden where Deborah was chatting with some of the other guests.

"Sorry, can I just interrupt everyone? This is Andrew."

Deborah stopped mid-conversation and took in the handsome man before her.

"I'll get you a beer, Andrew." With that, Bridget slipped away leaving her friends to get to know each other.

Back in the boardroom, David announced proudly, "I think our mission is complete. A special thanks to you, Cordelia, for coordinating everything."

"Oh, it was my pleasure, David, I can assure you," Cordelia cooed, her delphinium blue eyes sparkling mischievously.

By the end of the evening, Andrew and Deborah had arranged to meet the following day and as it was a Bank Holiday, Deborah had accepted Andrew's invitation to lunch and then a drive on to his rented barn for the weekend. It all felt incredibly comfortable between them and besides, neither of them had anything else planned, so they had nothing to lose.

When John and Bridget waved their friends off, who were now holding hands and smiling broadly, Bridget said, "You know, I'm sure somebody 'up there' is watching over you two."

Shadows

Shadows fall across the sunlit morn heavy with mist
Silence save for birdsong echoing in the trees; haunting,
Pecking my brain, drilling holes in my fortitude
A tug-of-war rope pulling me this way and that, nausea
Overwhelming me, the lure, the draw, the pull of the
Amber nectar swilled bilious and bloated as subliminal
Thoughts scatter-gun through my mind's eye and
My consciousness fights the realities of the day-to-day
Hum-drumming toils weighing me down like a lead weight
Dragging my body through the day, melancholic, robotic
Heaving my heavy heart with me, threatening to engulf me
In the pain that I wear pinned to my breast for all to see
Unravelling the minutiae of my life through the bottom of a
glass
Magnified in its glorious nectar-like nirvana state I grin with
glee
As I slake my thirst and satiate my never-ending need and greed
For the anaesthetic quality that I crave to make me numb again
To block out the sunlit morn heavy with mist
Silence

Castles in the Sand

It was the summer of 1976, the hottest for 350 years. The sand burned my feet as I scampered along Tenby Beach chasing a big, brightly coloured plastic beach ball. I was seventeen years old and couldn't have been happier.

Mum and Dad had joined Pete and me on the beach, a rare treat – taking a break from the farm did them good. I smiled across at them when I finally captured the ball; they were both snoozing in stripey deck chairs, knowing that I was keeping an eye on my younger siblings.

Millie and Greg were building sandcastles, Millie the workhorse collecting water from the fast receding shoreline, and Greg the architect, planning, building, and mapping out his grand castle design complete with moat and a driftwood bridge.

"Hey! Are you going to throw that thing over?" Pete called out, waving his arms. He was wearing black Speedos and standing on a tartan picnic blanket we had laid out earlier.

I ran back, tucking the ball under my arm, quickly jumping onto the rug.

"The sand's too hot to stand on! It's burning my feet," I said, surprised.

Afraid the beach ball would get scooped up by a passing breeze, I let the air out and folded it up, tucking it into my straw beach bag alongside me as I sat down on the blanket to join the man that I loved.

Pete draped his arm gently around my shoulders, which felt hot and slightly sore.

"Let me put some more sun cream on you, you'll burn otherwise."

I reached into my bag and pulled out some Hawaiian Tropic sun cream which smelt of coconuts and reminded me of a tropical beach. I handed it to Pete who rubbed some gently into my shoulders and back. He handed me the bottle back and I rubbed some into my chest, tummy and legs, before passing it back to him.

My skimpy shoe-string bikini barely covered my assets and I could see Pete admiring my tanned, taut body and I felt a pang of desire as he started rubbing the sun cream into his toned chest and abs. He was a good-looking guy and I adored him. We had been together for nine months and it felt like the real deal, but we were both young and there was no rush.

We laid down side by side and he took my hand in his as we lazed in the sun.

Dad had perked up after his snooze and was looking at his watch when I looked across at him a while later. Although it was still early, I knew that he and Mum would have to dash back to the farm in time to milk the cows. I was hoping to stay out late with Pete, who would drop me back home afterward, but it all depended on Mum and whether she could cope without me for the evening milking shift.

I could see them talking and Mum was nodding her head. I hated the constraints of living on a farm. I wasn't going to stay after my college course and had decided that I was going to leave home as soon as I could. I had a wanderlust sense of adventure and I wanted to explore the world. Hopefully, with Pete.

"We're going to have to start to pack up and head off home, love," Dad called over.

My heart sank. That meant that me and Pete would have to leave the beach too. I glanced at Pete and made a 'sorry' face and shrugged my shoulders.

"Why don't we stop off for a quick drink on the way back?" Pete suggested, standing up and shaking some sand off a towel with bright yellow mermaids on it.

Mum and Dad had a quick conflab and nodded. "OK, just a quick one, then."

By the time we had gathered up our stuff and rounded up Millie and Greg, who both looked as though they had been out in the sun for a bit too long, it was getting on for four o'clock. Usually, people would have been making a move but on this glorious Saturday in August, everybody looked set to stay for some time yet. I wished so much that Pete and I could have stayed but I had to do as I was told.

"Where are you parked?" Pete asked my dad.

"Up near the Castle Hotel. Where are you?"

"We parked outside my sister's house on Montrose Road. It's right across from the Castle Hotel. When we get back to the car, you can follow me if you like. I know a lovely little pub on the way back, it's called The Ship and Anchor. They serve great food too if you fancy a bite to eat."

I knew what Pete was doing and I smiled at him and mouthed 'thank you'. He was trying to prolong our time together and that just made me love him even more.

Dad didn't respond to the suggestion of a meal and merely said, "We'll see you back at the car then," as he herded Millie and Greg onto the track leading through the sand dunes, laden with beach paraphernalia. Mum had gone on ahead.

Wearing flip-flops, shorts, and a fresh white tee-shirt that I had popped on before leaving the beach, I loaded our things into the back of Pete's Hillman Imp and settled into the front seat, grateful for the furry seat covers protecting me from scorching the back of my legs. He turned the key in the ignition and fired the car up, the faint smell of Castrol GTX permeating my nostrils as the engine roared into life.

"Ah, here comes your dad," he announced, raising his hand in acknowledgment before manoeuvring the car expertly out from the tightly parked cars and driving quickly away.

"Oops, I'd better slow down with your dad following me…"

He smiled and his whole face lit up into a mischievous grin. He was wearing jeans and a white cheesecloth shirt and he looked absolutely gorgeous. He smelt great too: he was wearing Denim for Men that I had bought him for his birthday.

Rod Stewart blared out, "I am sailing, I am sailing, home again 'cross the sea," from the eight-track stereo that Pete had installed and the traffic eased as we turned off the mini roundabout to go up The Maudlins and headed out of the town.

Pete checked the rear-view mirror to see that Dad had taken the correct exit and he was pleased to see that we hadn't lost them.

As we drove up the hill listening to Rod booming out, "We are sailing," in his gravelly voice, Pete changed down a gear. From nowhere, a car appeared over the brow of the hill and I screamed. Everything happened so quickly; there was nowhere for Pete to go and nothing that anybody could do.

I heard a sickening crunch and felt warm and wet. Then silence. I was in terrible pain. My teeth were in agony and I couldn't see. I could hear Mum's voice and I sensed somebody at the side window. The door opened and she said, "Rosy! Are you alright? Oh, God, somebody, call an ambulance. Quick!"

I was drenched in blood. Dazed and stunned, surrounded by broken glass and twisted metal, I could hear sirens wailing in the distance.

Neither of us could move and I sensed that Pete was badly injured. I was in shock.

Firemen quickly got to work on cutting Pete out of the wreckage and I was lifted out and taken to a nearby ambulance where I was carefully laid onto a stretcher. Pete was laid out on the stretcher next to me and he reached across and took my hand in his.

"I love you," he whispered. And then his hand dropped.

The paramedics did their best to save him, but it was too late.

We Are One

Light shafted through sunlit gauze, billowing through
The mirror of my mind; pulsating rhythms of my heart
Drawing me closer to the nearness of you, how I long
For your touch, your love, your mind, your feel: you
To take me back to the fire-lit warmth of the need in me
Seeking truths beyond any dreams I ever had just to feel
The closeness combine with my soul as one, we melt
Into our oneness that can never be divided
We are one

To Have and To Hold

When Belinda walked into The Bluebell Inn on a fresh, spring morning, she was greeted by a handful of the regulars nodding and smiling courteously.

"Had a good run, has she?" Bert inquired, reaching down from his bar stool to pet Rusty, Belinda's springer spaniel.

Rusty's tongue lolled out of the side of her mouth as she sat panting and accepting Bert's rough pats and strokes happily, closing her big brown eyes in blissful appreciation.

"Yes, we walked over the top today. It was beautiful," Belinda replied, pulling up a chair near the window opposite the bar.

"Heel," she said firmly to Rusty when she felt that her dog had received enough attention. The spaniel obediently lay at her feet and rested her head on her paws, watching her owner without moving her head.

"Black coffee?" Kath, the jovial owner, and bartender inquired, a warm friendly smile on her kind, lived-in face.

"Yes, Kath. Thanks," Belinda replied, loosening her coat.

The village of Brockhampton had a population of under a thousand people and when Belinda and Greg had first moved into Yew Tree Cottage seven years ago as newlyweds, they fell in love with the place and were touched by the villagers' kindness in welcoming them into the fold. As newcomers, she thought they would have to work hard at becoming part of the

community but thankfully, they slotted right into place.

Greg had joined the Parish Council and she had helped set up a Youth Club in the Village Hall, which hadn't been easy, but she had enjoyed it all the same, despite some cheekier kids being a bit of a handful. Her teaching experience kicked in and she eventually gained the trust and respect of her flock of children.

"Greg working away again, love?" Kath asked as she brought the coffee over and set it in front of Belinda.

Belinda smiled weakly, her short, bobbed hair framing her pretty face. "Yes, he's over in Northampton this week. Back on Friday, though."

Kath gave her a knowing look. "He's doing it all for you, love. You know that, don't you?"

Belinda bit back the tears. Of course, she knew. But it didn't dim the ache that she felt for him when he was away.

Kath pulled out the old wooden bar chair opposite her friend.

"How are you doing, love?" she asked. "You can always talk to me, you know that, don't you?" she said in her soft Scottish burr.

Even though village life can seem like living in a fishbowl at times with busybodies twitching their net curtains at the merest hint of a scandal, the night an ambulance had pulled up outside Yew Tree Cottage with its blue lights flashing, the village drums beat faster than ever. Before sun-up, practically everybody knew that Belinda had been rushed into Westmoore Hospital and that she had been in the early stages of pregnancy, but people rallied around and wanted to know how she was doing. Nobody actually asked the question that was on everybody's mind.

"I'm fine, Kath. Really," she added, reassuring her friend. "Greg and I are going to try for another baby soon. We need to heal first."

"You can come and talk to me anytime you need to, OK?" Kath reached out and patted her hand gently before getting back to tending to her customers.

The ectopic pregnancy had taken Belinda completely by surprise. She had been shopping in Marks & Spencer when she felt the first stab of pain and thought something wasn't right. When she had returned home and put her feet up, she had felt slightly better and as Greg was working away, she had decided to take a bath and have an early night.

The stabbing pains that woke her in the early hours were horrendous and she only just managed to call 999 for an ambulance. She didn't remember much after that.

The first thing she remembered was a young nurse striding breezily into her room at the hospital with Greg hot on her heels, his handsome face etched with concern.

"Hey. Are you alright? What happened? Was it a miscarriage? The doctors were very vague and said they wanted to speak to both of us, together."

Greg took Belinda into his arms and that's when she broke down.

The Magic Kingdom

Ahmed sat cross-legged on the oriental rug pouring Arabic coffee from a Dallah into a small glass and handed it to his Western guest, who received it with a nod of his head, before sipping the hot, cardamom-laced liquid.

"So, Mr. Matthews, how many camels must I give you before you let me marry your wife?" he asked, the smell of his expensive Oud mingling with the aroma of the coffee. It was such an evocative, sophisticated smell and Paul always associated it with well-groomed, wealthy Arabs.

Ahmed laughed mischievously, his eyes glittering, his even white teeth bright against his olive skin, emphasising his handsome face.

"We can only have one wife in our country, Ahmed. You know that and Ellie is mine!" Paul said, firmly. He was never sure whether to take Ahmed seriously or not, but thankfully he knew that he was joking about wanting to barter for his wife, who worked in the same department as him at the hospital.

"Yes, I am only playing with you, but you should have seen your face!" he exclaimed.

Paul liked Ahmed and was honoured that he had invited him to his home, and had entered via the men's entrance so as not to encounter any of the female members of his family when he had arrived earlier.

"But I am looking for a second wife," Ahmed continued, nonchalantly, "and as you cannot – or will not – help me, I will keep looking." He sipped his coffee, holding the glass between his forefinger and thumb.

Paul smiled. He had worked with Ahmed at the Military Hospital in Jeddah for some years and was impressed with his impeccable English; it put his small selection of Arabic phrases to shame, even though he had lived in the Kingdom for almost six years.

The conversation turned to more serious matters and Ahmed asked the man sitting cross-legged opposite him whether he had heard anything about a bootlegging ring operating in the Kingdom. Paul was careful not to impart what he had heard on the ex-pat grapevine because it was only supposition and gossip. He hoped that what he had heard was just that: gossip. If not, his good friend, Chuck, could be in deep trouble.

Skilfully, he steered the conversation away and on to the lighter subject of where it was possible to buy the incredibly expensive Oud that Ahmed wore. He thought he might even treat himself to some, one day.

To round the evening off, the men chatted about a couple of projects that they were involved with at the hospital before the call for Isha prayer meant that Paul knew that it was time to go, and he bid his colleague farewell with a firm handshake and a smile.

As he drove along the busy four-lane Al Malek Road back to the Western compound where he and Ellie lived, Paul put a Phil

Collins tape into the stereo of his company Cadillac and his thoughts turned to their upcoming holiday to The Maldives. They hadn't had a break in months and the long days and five-and-a-half-day working weeks were taking their toll, not to mention the oppressive heat and humidity, but their increasingly fattening bank accounts were compensation enough and the reason they had chosen to live half-way around the world, far from their family and friends.

Pulling in through the gated entrance to the compound, the guard greeted Paul with a friendly wave and a smile, "Good evening, sir," and then lifted the barrier to let him through. He smiled and waved back before driving slowly over the numerous speed bumps until he reached the furthest section of the compound and parked neatly in one of the bays allocated to the Cordoba residents.

Ellie was reading a book by the pool and when she saw Paul, she got up from her lounger and accompanied him into their villa.

"Are you alright?" Paul asked, seeing her slightly clouded expression.

"I'll tell you inside," she replied cryptically.

Once inside the villa, she turned to Paul in the large, open-plan lounge/diner and said, "Charlene rang me from Florida earlier. She can't get hold of Chuck and she's really worried."

"What? What do you mean?" he said, laying his car keys on the coffee table.

Paul sat down on one of the cream-coloured sofas and crossed his ankle over his knee taking in what his wife had just told him.

"Wasn't he flying to Riyadh today for some big meeting?" he quizzed.

"I don't know. Charlene left yesterday, exit-only, but Chuck was staying on for a couple of months to 'tie up some loose ends' – I assume with his work contract?" Ellie surmised.

"How did Charlene sound?"

"Upset and really worried. Why do you ask?"

"I can't say, Ellie. You have to trust me on this one."

"Hey! I'm your wife, for goodness' sake. What's going on?" she demanded.

Paul got up and walked to the square beige push-button telephone on the TV cabinet, ignoring his wife's question.

"What's going on, Paul?"

"I don't know! Let me think. Go and pour me a Scotch, will you?"

Ellie sensed her husband's unease and obediently poured two fingers of Jack Daniels into a heavy cut-glass tumbler, which she placed on the coffee table in the lounge area. She thought about pouring herself one but decided against it; the bottle of Jack Daniels had been a gift from Chuck to Paul and it was as rare as hen's teeth.

When she and Paul had first arrived in Saudi, she quickly discovered that most ex-pats have access to alcohol and as long as they drank it behind closed doors on their compounds, a blind eye was generally turned. However, she also knew that it was prohibited in the Kingdom and was always careful, just like the rest of the expatriate community, because they knew they could face hundreds of lashings, deportation, fines or even imprisonment if they were caught drinking or in possession of alcohol.

Paul made some phone calls while Ellie prepared for bed. When she came back down from upstairs wearing a knee-length silk robe, Paul was on his second tumbler of whisky which was half-full.

"What's going on, Paul?" she asked, her voice full of concern.

"Chuck seems to have vanished off the face of the earth," he said solemnly, staring at the glass in front of him.

"What do you mean? He's probably with some mates somewhere. You know what he's like…"

Paul took a slug from his glass and winced.

"Go to bed, Ellie."

Sensing something was seriously wrong, she reluctantly turned around and went back upstairs.

Three days later, there was still no news of Chuck either on the ex-pat grapevine or from his wife back in Florida.

Paul had a clandestine meeting with Chuck's trusted colleague, Randy, who was also in the dark about his friend's whereabouts, although they both had their suspicions: buried in the desert with a hole in his head.

There was little they could do to find him and the company Chuck worked for had even approached the authorities, as well

as checked with all the hospitals in the area, in case he had been involved in a road traffic accident.

Stories circulated regularly among the ex-pat community about Siddiqui stills or fake passports because there will always be those who choose to take the low road to earn a fast buck when an opportunity presents itself. Sadly, it seemed that Chuck had fallen into this category.

Ellie and Paul had a long talk and decided that it was time to call it a day and repatriate to the U.K.

Chuck's disappearance had rattled them and they applied for their exit-only visas and organised the packers to come into their villa and pack up their six years of life in the 'magic Kingdom'. They hosted a Ma Salama party by the pool outside their villa and thanked their ex-pat buddies for being such good friends to them; they had had a wonderful time and would be sad to leave.

Six weeks later, when they were unpacking their shipment from Saudi into their country cottage in Hampshire, there was a knock on the door. Paul went to answer it.

It was a man with a package addressed to Mr. Paul Matthews.

"What is it? Ellie asked, curiously.

"How should I know? I haven't opened it yet."

"You haven't ordered anything, then?"

"Nope."

In among the copious amounts of packaging finally appeared a small bottle of Oud, accompanied by a note:

May your kindness brush up against all those who meet you and have the pleasure of working with you. I was sorry to hear about your friend, Chuck. I cannot be seen to get involved but I will try to put in a good word for him at the prison.

Take care, my friend.

Ahmed

ABOUT THE AUTHOR

Rosy Gee was born in West Sussex but grew up on a smallholding in Surrey. She travelled extensively, living and working in the Middle East for many years before settling back down in rural England in later life to pursue her life-long ambition of becoming a full-time writer and novelist. This is her debut collection of poetry and short stories and she is already working on her next volume.

Printed in Great Britain
by Amazon